Roser Capdevila • Anne-Laure Fournier le Ray

Grandparents!

Kane/Miller
BOOK PUBLISHERS

First American Edition 2003 by Kane/Miller Book Publishers
La Jolla, California

Originally published in France as
Des grands-parents, quelle aventure!
@ Bayard Presse/Pomme d'Api
@2001 Bayard Editions Jeunesse

Library of Congress Control Number: 2002113163

Printed and bound in Singapore by Tien Wah Press, (Pte.) Ltd.

1 2 3 4 5 6 7 8 9 10

ISBN 1-929321-46-8

This book is for all children who are lucky

enough to have grandparents,

and for all grandparents who are

lucky enough to have grandchildren.

To _____

With love from _____

All Grandparents hav

Some have well-known, popular names,

Grandma

Grandpa

some have long names,

Little Grandmother

Grandfather from Canada

some have cutsie names,

Grampy

Granny

eir own names.

some have funny names,

Popsie

Gran-Nan

some have formal names,

Grandmother

Grandfather

and some have names we gave them when we were babies.

Pop-Pop

Nana

… it's been so long, that we can't even remember the first time we met them.

But they remember everything…

We usually recognize them.

And we never, ever, get ***them*** confused!

Some grandparents are very good at explaining just exactly who is who.

But most have to repeat themselves over and over until we really get it.

There are some children who are able to understand right away.

And there are others who need to have a picture drawn.

There are some grandparents
who are a little mysterious.

So, we ask questions, and then
we learn more about them.

There are some who are
too serious to be a lot of fun.

So, we have to teach them.

There are some who seem to know everything.

But we can still surprise them.

There are those who
forget everything...

...except the most
important things.

Some don't
hear very well...

... but some hear
all too well.

Some seem very old.

Some think we are very amusing.

Some have beards;

others don't have
much hair at all.

Some are young;

others are very old.

Some like to stay home;

others like to go out.

Some wear glasses;

others wear hats.

Some are very strict;

others are easygoing.

And sometimes there is one who is our favorite.

Sometimes they come to our house.

They come if our parents are going to be late from work,

or if our parents are going out at night.

randparents in different places.

Sometimes we go to theirs.

At some grandparents' houses, we can't touch anything.

At others, there are secret play spots.

Most of the time, it's very different from our own house!

We might learn how to cook.

We might learn how to whistle

We might learn how to use
the computer.

We might learn how to fish.

Lots of times we get to see our cousins there.
They are kind of like brothers and sisters, except they're
less annoying because we don't see them as often.

There are some who work all day.

Others have retired, but are still very pressed for time.

Some have a little free time, but get tired easily.

Others have nothing but time, and lots of ideas.

There are some who live far away,
so we hardly ever get to see them.

Sometimes we talk to them on the phone
or send letters.

nd some we never see.

Sadly, there are some who have died.

Everyone has their own way of remembering them.

There are some who tell us about our parents when they were little.

This was your father's favorite bear.

You know, she talks to me during the night.

There are some with whom we share our deepest secrets.

f family things.

Some of them tell us
true stories.

Others tell us
made-up stories.

And some tell stories that are
half true and half made-up.

There are some who are always on our side.

There are some who are always there to make us feel better.

There are some who like to fool around.

And some with whom we plan big surprises.

We grow up with them ...

Sometimes they need our help.

They give us compliments.

They invite us out.

And we invite them out, too.

but we get to stay little, too.

We don't always have to be doing something when we're with our grandparents.

We feel warm and cozy in our grandparents' arms.

All in all, grandparents are very important!

It's because of them that we get together as a family. It's because of them that we are a family!